Sophie's Spe

By Sarah Griffiths

Illustrated by Lisa Williams

© Copyright 2018 Sarah Griffiths
First Published 2018

ISBN 978-1-9999758-2-1

TEAMAUTHOR UK
Publishing with you

This Book Belongs to:

....

Dedication
For children all over the world. May you discover your own inner beauty and wisdom.

xxx

Sophie was a 7-year-old,
A happy, bright young girl,
She worked so hard to try her best,
But her mind was in a whirl.

Sophie wanted to be just perfect,
At everything she tried,
She worked so hard and got upset,
But her best was always inside.

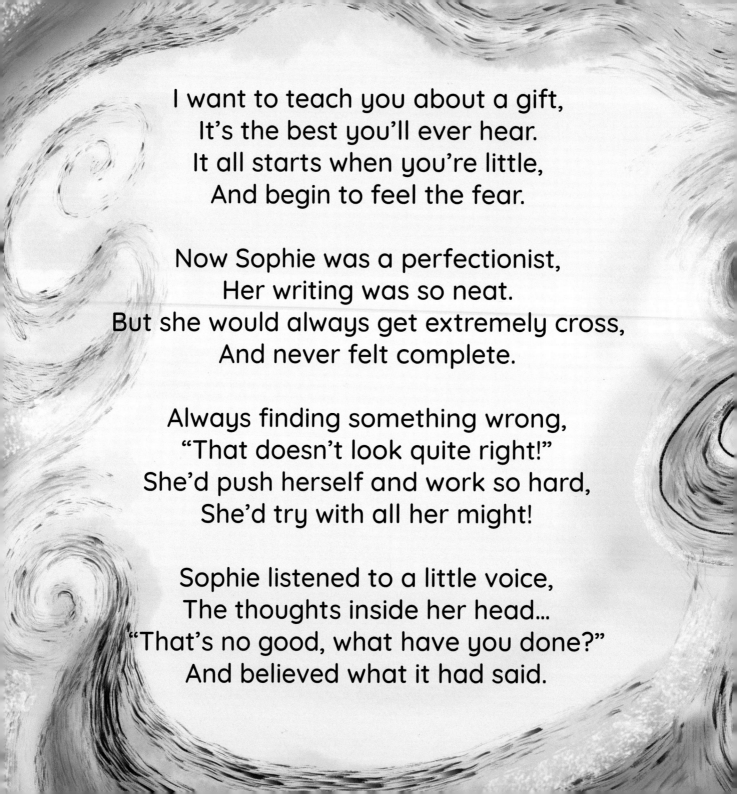

I want to teach you about a gift,
It's the best you'll ever hear.
It all starts when you're little,
And begin to feel the fear.

Now Sophie was a perfectionist,
Her writing was so neat.
But she would always get extremely cross,
And never felt complete.

Always finding something wrong,
"That doesn't look quite right!"
She'd push herself and work so hard,
She'd try with all her might!

Sophie listened to a little voice,
The thoughts inside her head…
"That's no good, what have you done?"
And believed what it had said.

The lesson I will teach you,
Will make you jump for joy,
Get off your seat and shout HOORAY!
Every girl and boy.

It really will set you free,
Please share it far and wide.
You'll be the best that you can be,
Feel happy on the inside.

When you see with clarity,
This secret becomes clear,
You'll fly so high and reach your dreams,
There is nothing else to fear.

It all started one day in Class 2,
Sophie was feeling stressed.
The voice in her head, on overdrive,
She didn't feel her best.

Class 2 had a supply teacher,
But only for the day.
When she walked into the room,
She had something inspiring to say.

"My name is Miss Cookie,"
She said with sparkling eyes.
A friendly face with dimples,
And lines that made her wise.

"Today is a celebration,
We all have a chance to shine.
I'll go first and demonstrate,
And you all get in line."

Sophie felt dread inside!
"I don't know what to do?"
She looked around at all her friends,
And joined the back of the queue.

Emily read a poem,
She knew it off by heart.
Such confidence and self-belief,
She gave right from the start.

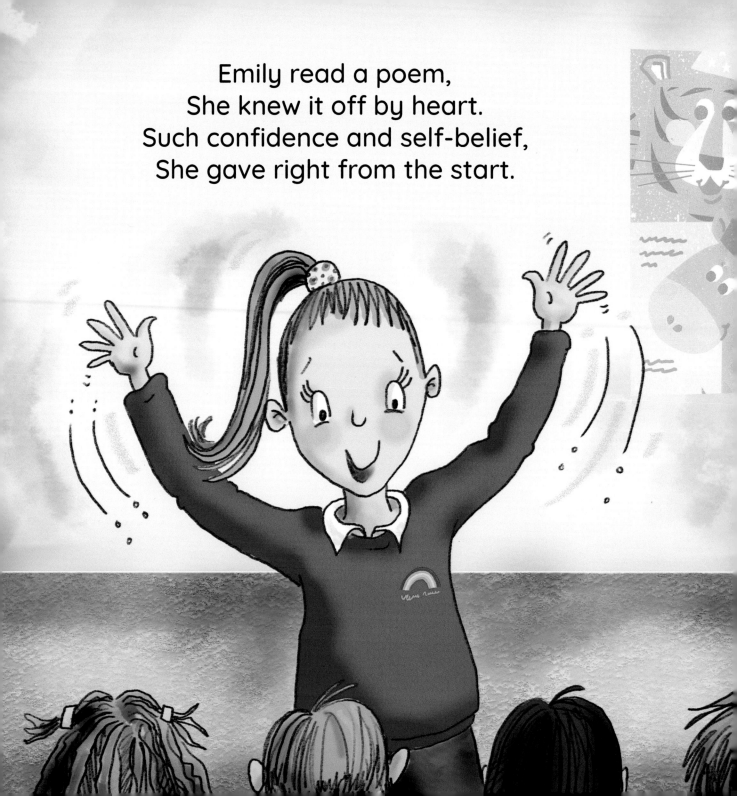

Next in turn was sporty Sam,
Captain of the football team.
He played for Wolves Under 10s,
This really was his dream.

"Your turn George," Miss Cookie said.
He began to tell a story,
He changed his voice for characters,
And shone in all his glory.

As more and more of Sophie's class,
Performed for all to see,
Sophie became anxious and said,
"They are so much better than me!"

Next came Jack, Alexandra too,
Marcus and then Molly.
They all had something different to share,
Then came Joe and Holly.

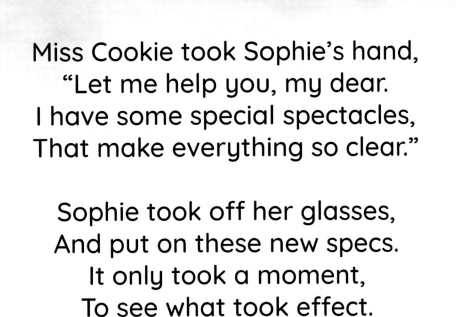

Miss Cookie took Sophie's hand,
"Let me help you, my dear.
I have some special spectacles,
That make everything so clear."

Sophie took off her glasses,
And put on these new specs.
It only took a moment,
To see what took effect.

As Sophie held the spectacles
And placed them around her ears,
What she saw was magnificent,
The fear then disappeared.

She saw in all its splendour,
A truly wonderous sight.
All her friends lit up the room,
With an inner guiding light.

Auras dazzling around them,
Pulsing in rhythm and glowing.
The energy field so powerful,
Was connected to them and flowing.

The glasses had given Sophie a gift,
They opened a new dimension.
They took away the worry she felt,
And all of the terrible tension.

Sophie looked into the window,
And what she saw in her reflection,
Was the beauty from within,
That shone back in the projection!

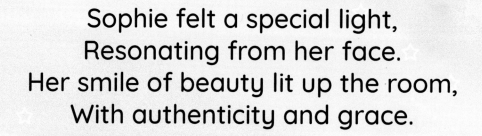

Sophie felt a special light,
Resonating from her face.
Her smile of beauty lit up the room,
With authenticity and grace.

Sophie talked about her friends,
And about her family,
About the bond with others,
Her strength for all to see.

She realised that with these specs,
It made it plain for all.
Sophie's kindness was her gift,
Which made her stand so tall.

As Sophie looked at her class,
She felt their inner flame.
Georgie, Grace, Tom and Sam,
She would never be the same!

The glasses see what we can't see,
It's invisible to the eye.
But when you feel the energy,
Your self-esteem will fly!

It feels like a vibration,
Energy moving from within,
Realising our true potential,
Sends our universe into a spin.

We all have gifts that make us shine,
All different from one another.
We must believe we are good enough,
And celebrate each other.

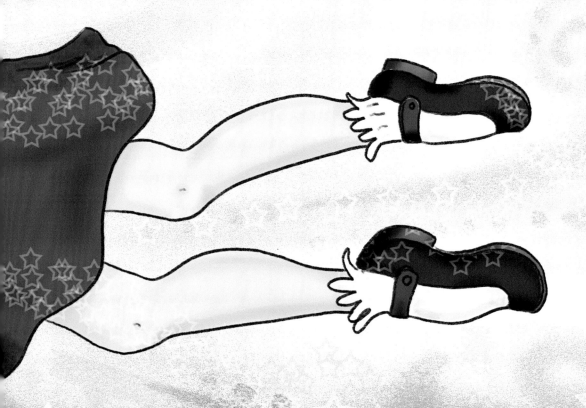

So, Sophie was given special specs,
To make her understand,
We can do anything we choose to do,
It's all in our own hands.

Believe in yourself, aim so high,
Give your gifts to all.
Make it count, this is your time,
One life, so stand up tall!

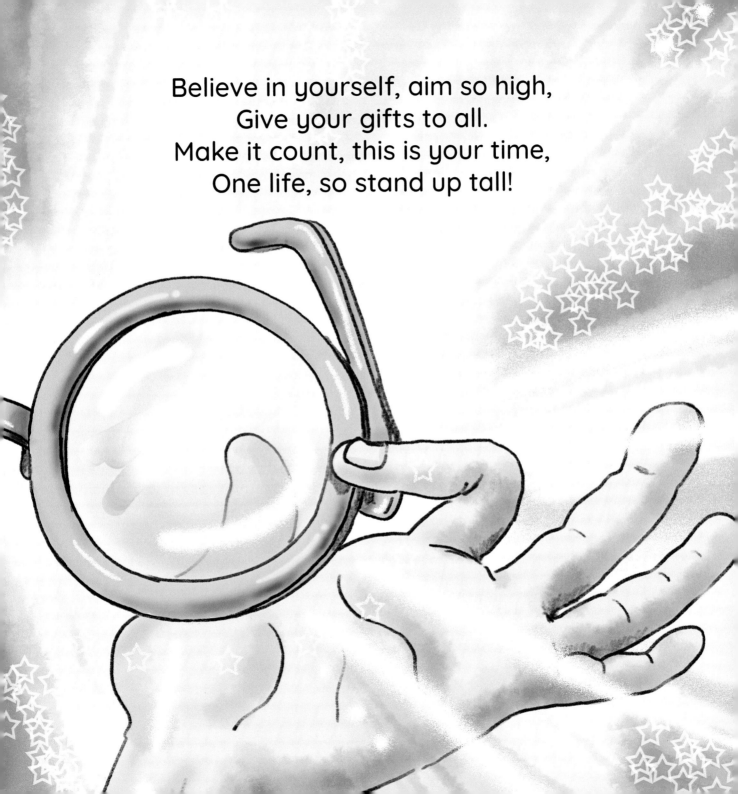

About the Author

Sarah has a great passion for children's writing and storytelling. She has been writing for children for over 10 years. Sarah is an experienced teacher and has taught children in Primary Schools for over 11 years.

Sarah is a children's author and holds author visits at schools, nurseries and libraries. Stories are brought to life with special props and a special storytelling performance from Sarah! Together with her stories, she also teaches story writing, creative writing, poetry and self-esteem workshops that are inspired from her books. Sarah is very passionate about championing children to transform their self-esteem. Through her stories, Sarah's mission is to celebrate children's uniqueness, uncover their dreams, their passions and embrace their strengths. Her special message is:

"We are all magnificent and can reach our dreams, if we can just change the way we think."

To follow Sarah and find out more about her books, please visit:
www.sarahgriffithsauthor.co.uk

f @SarahGriffithsAuthor

🐦 @SarahGriffithsA

About the Illustrator

Lisa Williams decided to be an illustrator whilst she was still in primary school. She has been illustrating children's books, magazines and educational material for nearly 25 years.

Whilst taking on commercial work, Lisa took a teacher training course, but since qualifying, her commercial success has been such that she hasn't had the time to teach! Lisa is one of the talented illustrators for TeamAuthorUK. This allows her the opportunity to work with a variety of authors and develop an array of styles.

For more information, visit Lisa's Facebook page:
f @lisawilliamsillustration

Acknowledgements

Thank you to my husband Martyn, my daughter Eva, my family and friends for all your love and support.

Thank you to the incredibly talented Lisa Williams for your exceptional illustrations. Sophie and the other characters are based on children I used to teach. Thank you for bringing to life the real magic of inner beauty to my story with your artistic excellence!

Thank you to Sue Miller for all your help, support and advice to publish this very special book.

Thank you to all the team at Team Author UK for your help and support.

Testimonial

"Sarah Griffiths' "Sophie's Spectacles" is an uplifting gift of empowerment and self-esteem elevation for children.
Every child deserves to have a copy to remind them of their inherent magnificence when they forget."

Dr. Joe Rubino
Creator of www.highselfesteemkids.com and
www.highselfesteemadults.com

Thank you to the sponsors of "Sophie's Spectacles"

Sophie's Spectacles is part of an international sponsorship project to transform children's self-esteem. The generosity of local businesses will help the author to spread an important message to the world: "We are all magnificent and we can do anything we desire, if we can just change the way we think!"

Sarah Griffiths would like to personally thank:

Vinay Najran and Rizwaan Makda	Andy Rao	Sue Miller
Specsavers Telford	**Key 3 Media**	**Team Author UK**

Michael Barrett - **Michael Barrett Financial Services**
Paul Delahay - **Tutor Doctor Telford**
Lorna McCann - **Lorna McCann PR**
Phyl Edmonds - **Severn Intervention Services**
Fay Strangwood - **Ironbridge Training Consultants**

10% of the funds raised for the project are donated to:

Partnership for Children is a UK registered charity that helps children to be mentally and emotionally healthy – just as exercise, good food and sleep help them to be physically healthy.